Annabelle the Angler Fish

Children's Picture Book by Montana DeBor

安娜貝爾琵琶魚

兒童插畫書

蒙泰娜・黛波兒　著

立宏義　譯

Dedicated to all the funny fish in the sea...

謹以此書獻給所有海洋中的滑稽魚兒…

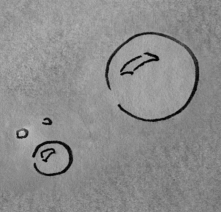

Annabelle the Angler Fish was the funniest looking fish in the deep, blue sea,

安娜貝爾琵琶魚是深藍的深海中最滑稽的魚兒，

With teeth like scissors and eyes of black ebony.

她的牙齒像剪刀，黑黑的似檀木的雙眼。

Her fins were pointy and her lips were full.
She swam with the grace of a stumbling bull.

她的鰭尖尖，她的嘴唇厚厚。
她的游泳姿態有如一隻蹣跚的大笨牛。

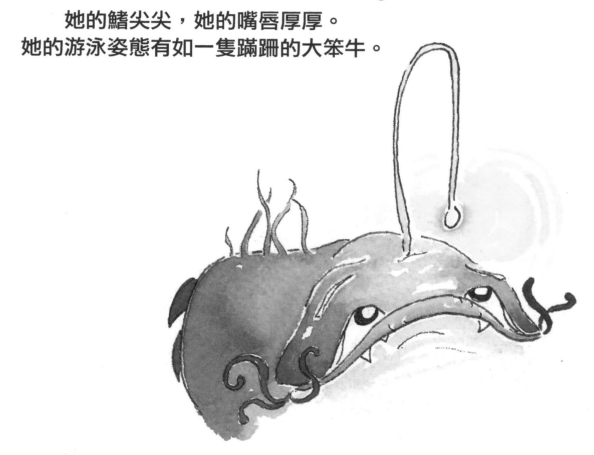

The other fish laughed and the other fish jested,
In beauty Annabelle could easily be bested.

有些魚兒訕笑她，有些魚兒嘲弄她，
她的容貌實在令人不敢恭維。

"You're in need of a dentist and your body goes squish!
We're so much prettier than you!"
said the smug jellyfish.

得意洋洋的水母說：
「　妳應該去給牙醫師整整牙，
妳的身材簡直是一塌糊塗！
我們比妳不知道要漂亮多少呢！　」

"Where are your tentacles?"
asked the octopi,

「妳的觸鬚在那裡？」章魚們問。

As they frowned upon Annabelle while swimming by.

當魚兒們游過安娜貝爾時，他們都不斷地皺眉頭。

And last but not least splashed along
a school of sardines,
"We thought you looked bad,
you're worse to sniff than be seen!"
最後，
成群結隊的沙丁魚也潑水游來湊熱鬧：
「　我們覺得妳長得真醜，
可是妳聞起來卻更糟糕！　」

Annabelle felt sad and
looked down in shame,

安娜貝爾傷心極了，
低下頭來，覺得好丟臉。

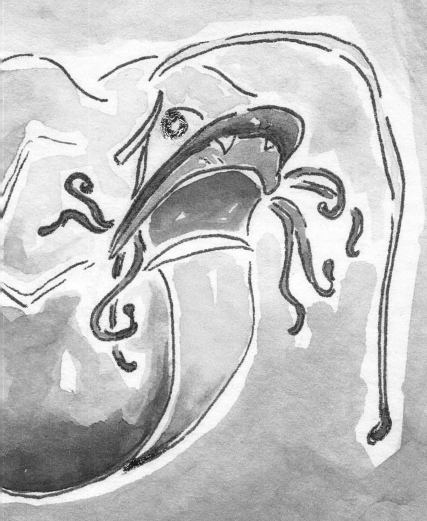

At her fins and her teeth and her long spikey mane.

看著自己的背鰭、

牙齒加上長而尖尖的鬃刺，

越看越傷心。

"But I have something no other fish has!"
Exclaimed Annabelle who now felt very glad.

突然天外飛來一筆，
安娜貝爾大聲歡呼起來：

「啊！
我有其它的魚兒
沒有的東西！」

She was confident as she swam away,
"I'll know what to do the next time
those fish come to play"

她一面游出去，
一面覺得信心滿滿。
「我知道下回怎麼對付這些魚兒了。」

The next morning the harassing
sea creatures came back,
To mock Annabelle about the beauty
she lacked.

次日早晨，

這些會騷擾的魚兒們回來了，

又想去戲弄嘲笑安娜貝爾缺少的麗姿，

But they looked and they
looked from the cove to the beach,
And swam down deep
where the sunlight didn't reach.

他們找來找去，

從小灣找到海灘，

游來游去，游到太陽照不到的深海處。

The bullying fish reached the ocean's floor,
Where they noticed a glowing light they hadn't before.

這些喜歡霸凌的魚兒們一直游到海床深處，
看到了以前從來沒見過的一個閃閃的光。

"Ooh, so pretty! What's this?"
said the fish as they swam toward the glow.

「多美呀！這是甚麼？」
他們一面七嘴八舌地問，一面游向這光。

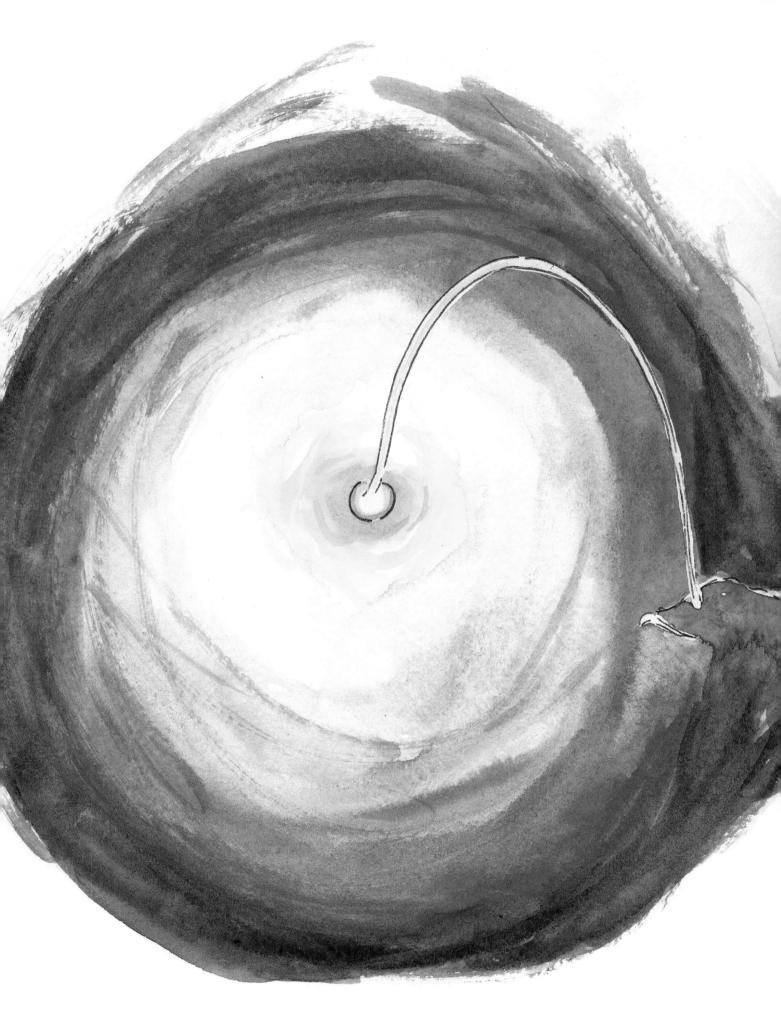

"I'm not sure, let's go inside, it looks like...uh oh!"

「啊，我不知道是甚麼，
我們一起進去瞧瞧，
啊呀！看起來像…呵呵，啊～～～」

Before they could turn and swim,
Annabelle shut her teeth in a wide smug grin.

他們還來不及會意轉身游出去時，

安娜貝爾把上下牙齒一合攏，

臉上露出自鳴得意與喜孜孜的笑容。

"So you like the look of my fishing light

but not me?

Too bad that's the last thing you'll ever see!"

「哈！你們喜歡的可是我釣魚的餌光

而不是我本尊喔？

糟的是，這可是你們眼中的最後一瞥喔！」

"Let us out, we're sorry, we shouldn't poke fun!"
Yelped the jellyfish from inside Annabelle's gums.

水母在安娜貝爾的牙床裡急得哇哇叫：
「請放過我們，對不起，我們不應該這樣戲弄你！」

So Annabelle thought and Annabelle pondered,
"Have they learned their lesson?"

she wondered.

安娜貝爾想了又想，
考慮再三，
她捫心自問：
「他們真的有得到了
教訓嗎？」

She unclenched her tee

"I hope you've learned n

她把合起的牙張開，

「我希望你

不要再以嘲弄為樂

"We're sorry. Lead us bac

Asked the octopus to whic

「我們真的知道錯了，現在請你

章魚苦苦哀求，安娜貝爾回答

and out tumbled the fish,
to tease, that's my wish!"

些魚兒們紛紛滾跌游出。

學到了規矩，
！這是我的願望！」

o the surface with your glow?"
nnabelle replied, "Yes, let's go."

你的光把我們帶到水面上去好嗎？」
「好吧，我帶你們一起游上去！」

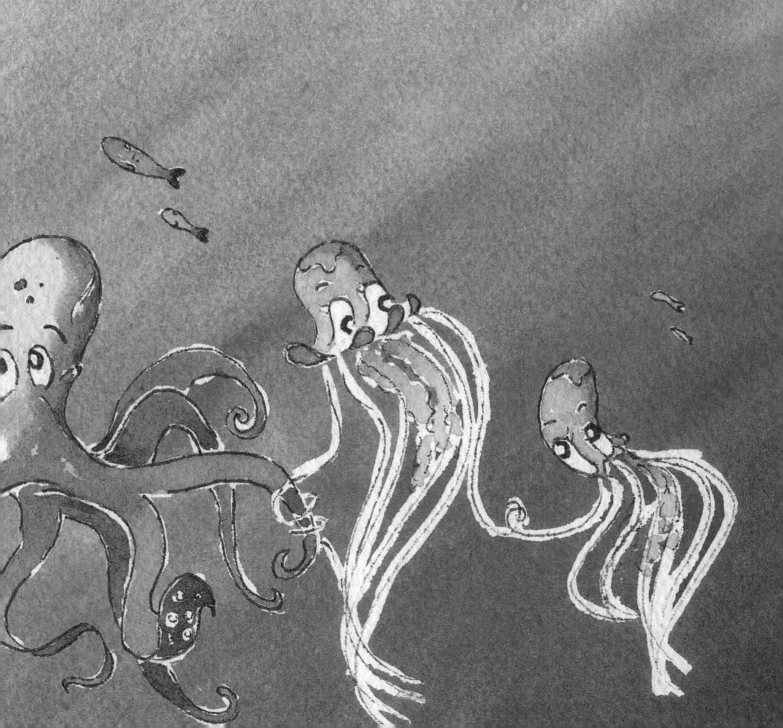

So she led them to safety and they all swam away,
Except for one sardine that stayed just to say,
"You're as pretty as the rest of us
in your own unique way!"

她就把魚兒們帶到安全地帶，其他的魚兒都游開了，

只有一條小沙丁魚
留下來說了一句話：
「妳就和我們一樣美麗，
因為妳有自己獨特的美！」

"Thank you"
said Annabelle as she looked at her angler's lure all aglow,
"I'm the prettiest fish in the deep blue sea.
I know!"

「多謝您。」
安娜貝爾一面說，一面朝自己琵琶魚特有的餌光看。
「我知道我是深深的藍海中最美麗的魚！」

The End

終

《安娜貝爾琵琶魚》故事情節介紹：

　　安娜貝爾琵琶魚是海洋世界中最滑稽的魚兒。她住在海底深處，有一個能吸引其它魚的光──彷彿就像魚餌。因為她古怪的外型，其它的海洋生物（包括水母，章魚，沙丁魚）都不斷嘲笑她。可是當這些魚兒在海底迷路後，安娜貝爾決定給他們一個教訓，偷偷地把他們困住；當她認為這些驚嚇的魚兒們已經得到了教訓後，她便釋放他們並好心地把大家領回安全的海域。安娜貝爾之所以這樣做，就是要用一己之力給這些魚兒們一個機會教育，要他們不可以霸凌與他們不同類的魚種。本國際版插畫書大量以英語修辭押韻抒發故事，即便中文譯文有不同韻味，仍無損其故事的原創精神與教育理念。雙語版的童書插圖來自作者個人創作的全彩水彩畫及水墨畫，生動地演繹描述這些海洋中的生物及它們的棲居地。

A brief plot line for "Annabelle the Angler Fish" :

Annabelle the Angler Fish is the funniest looking fish around. She lives near the ocean floor and possesses a glowing fishing lure. The other sea creatures (including jellyfish, octopi, and sardines) tease her for her odd appearance. However when those fish become lost at the bottom of the sea Annabelle decides to teach them a lesson by sneaking up and trapping them. However she feels they've learned their lesson and she releases them. She guides them to safety and in doing so teaches the fish not to bully and to accept others' differences. The illustrations are colorful watercolor and ink paintings of the sea creatures and their marine habitat.

蒙泰娜‧黛波兒出生與成長在美國維吉尼亞州的阿靈頓城（緊鄰首都華盛頓），從小對藝術產生濃厚的興趣並且展開繪畫學習，十歲開過個人水彩畫展，所有畫作一賣而空，自此，蒙泰娜開始經常在地方畫廊舉辦水彩畫展的創作。期間長達七年之久，蒙泰娜參與多次得獎的地方電視節目「阿靈頓的藝術」並擔任節目主持人，在這每月一播的節目中，她有機會訪問許多本土藝術家，包含彫塑家到演員、肚皮舞表演女郎與捏塑壽司的廚師，蒙泰娜儼然成為大華盛頓區文化及藝術的推手。

　　蒙泰娜積極參與各種創新的藝術媒體，她學過小提琴並在音樂會中表演多年，並且熱情融入許多地方戲劇的演出、導演服務與表演藝術工作。2010年起擔任伊利沙白大廈的常任藝術家，並在藝術工作坊中擔任義工，以藝術影響那些無家可歸的問題青少年與其母親；2011年起在維吉尼亞州立大學喬治‧梅森 GWU 的校園報擔任政治議題漫畫家。蒙泰娜最近密集展開個人畫展，展出地點包含華盛頓會議中心、喬治鎮冬宮美術館、藝術球、華盛頓大學畫廊及亞歷山大學院之畫廊藝術館。這是她第一本為華文世界所繪的兒童插畫書。

Montana DeBor was born and raised in Arlington, Virginia and has had an interest in art from the beginning. She started studying drawing at a young age and had her first watercolor show when she was ten years old. It sold out. Since then she has had many other watercolor exhibitions in local galleries. She created and hosted the awardwinning, local television program, "Arlington in Art" for seven years. In the monthly show she interviewed local artists ranging from sculptors and actors to belly dancers and sushi chefs in order to promote art and culture in the Washington, D.C. area.

Montana has been very involved in other mediums of art as well. She has studied and performed the violin for many years. She has also been very involved in theater; directing and acting in local shows.

She began her position of Artist in Residence for the Elizabeth House, part of Borromeo Housing, in 2010. She teaches volunteer art workshops and art therapy to the homeless teen moms in the program. She began her position as political cartoonist for the GWU Hatchet Newspaper in 2011. She most recently exhibited at the Washington Convention Center, Winter Palace Gallery in Georgetown, Artisphere, UCDC Gallery, and Alexandria Lyceum. This is her first book published for Chinese children.

科學小百科

　　琵琶魚俗稱**鮟鱇魚**，主要的特徵還是在非常奇特的第一背鰭，它的頭部的前邊的吻觸鬚末端通常有發光器，用來吸引其它的魚過來，因此也叫做燈籠魚。

美國國家地理雜誌提供

安娜貝爾琵琶魚
Annabelle the Angler Fish

作　　者／蒙泰娜．黛波兒

翻　　譯／丘宏義博士

美　　編／趙康芸

出 版 者／美商 EHGBooks 微出版公司

發 行 者／漢世紀數位文化（股）公司

　　　　　臺灣學人出版網：http://www.TaiwanFellowship.org

　　　　　住址／ 106 台北市大安區敦化南路 2 段 1 號 4 樓

　　　　　電話／ 02-2707-9001 轉 616-617

印　　刷／漢世紀數位文化（股）公司古騰堡®數位出版 POD 雲端科技

出版日期／ 2012 年 12 月（亞馬遜 Kindle 電子書同步出版）

總 經 銷／ Amazon.com

台灣銷售網／三民網路書店：http://www.sanmin.com.tw

　　　　　三民書局復北店

　　　　　　地址／ 104 台北市復興北路 386 號

　　　　　　電話／ 02-2500-6600

　　　　　三民書局重南店

　　　　　　地址／ 100 台北市重慶南路一段 61 號

　　　　　　電話／ 02-2361-7511

　　　　　全省金石網路書店：http://www.kingstone.com.tw

定　　價／新臺幣 400 元（美金 13.99 元／人民幣 90 元）

CPSIA information can be obtained
at www.ICGtesting.com
Printed in the USA
LVIC06n1909180814
399709LV00006B/85